ORCA
YOUNG
READERS

Belle
of Batoche

Jacqueline Guest

ORCA BOOK PUBLISHERS

Library and Archives Canada Cataloguing in Publication

Guest, Jacqueline
Belle of Batoche / Jacqueline Guest.
(Orca young readers)

ISBN 978-1-55143-297-7

1. Batoche (Sask.), Battle of, 1885--Juvenile fiction. I. Title. II. Series.
PS8563.U365B44 2004   jc813'.54   C2004-905172-5

Library of Congress Control Number: 2004112452

Summary: Belle must put aside her struggle to become the church bell ringer when those she loves are threatened during the battle of Batoche, part of the Riel Rebellion.

MIX
Paper from
responsible sources
FSC® C016245

Orca Book Publishers is dedicated to preserving the environment and has printed this book on Forest Stewardship Council® certified paper.

Orca Book Publishers gratefully acknowledges the support for its publishing programs provided by the following agencies: the Government of Canada through the Canada Book Fund and the Canada Council for the Arts, and the Province of British Columbia through the BC Arts Council and the Book Publishing Tax Credit.

Cover & interior illustrations by June Lawrason

ORCA BOOK PUBLISHERS
PO Box 5626, Stn. B
Victoria, BC Canada
V8R 6S4

ORCA BOOK PUBLISHERS
PO Box 468
Custer, WA USA
98240-0468

www.orcabook.com
Printed and bound in Canada.

17 16 15 14 • 8 7 6 5

For the grade three and four Time Twisters
of Louis Riel Elementary School, Calgary:
students who really did make history come alive!

And for their extraordinary teachers,
Sandy Langford, Tim Shoults and Jane Spratt.

A real class act!

Village of Batoche

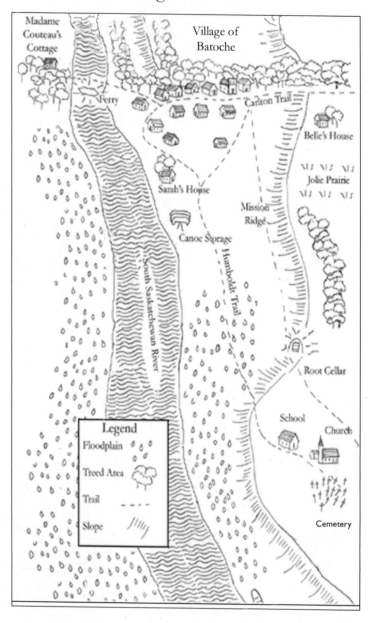

Table of Contents

1

Unexpected Competition

Belle emerged from the warm blackness of the old chicken coop into the blinding April sunshine.

"Belle Tourond, where are you, ma fille?"

Belle had stopped to watch an early robin busily building a nest in a poplar tree and now she was late again. Spring was very late coming this year, and Belle felt sorry for the birds trying to make nests in the leafless trees.

Sighing, she blew a puff of air up into her straight black hair and watched as a feather came loose, drifting down onto the frosty early morning ground. Time had a way of slipping away from Belle; at least that's what her mama always said.

Grown-ups had a different idea of how time should be spent, Belle thought. Instead of stopping to enjoy the first crocus of the year or to watch a fish jump in the river, adults were always rushing here and there with chores.

Today, Belle had spent a short time, she was sure it had been only a very short time, spying on a sweet little robin building a nest. What harm could there be in that?

She set the basket of eggs she'd been gathering onto a fence post where it teetered while she wiped her grimy hands on the apron of her long dress. "Coming Mama!" she called, grabbing the basket just in time.

Belle lived in the small town of Batoche in the area of the North West Territories called Saskatchewan. The town was on the Carlton Trail, the main trade route between Fort Garry and Fort Edmonton.

She glanced up at the wide-open prairie sky. It was like looking into a vast blue ocean, or at least what she imagined an ocean

would look like. She had never seen anything bigger than the South Saskatchewan
River, which she thought was very impres-
sive, especially during spring run off.
Batoche was built on the banks of the
South Saskatchewan and boasted a real
ferryboat that took people and freight from
bank to bank.

"It took me a little longer than usual today,
Mama. I had to wrestle a couple of those
hens before they'd give up their darned old
eggs!" Belle said as she hustled into the
back porch.

"Oui, I think it took a little longer because
you stopped to watch a tree growing leaves!
I swear your head is so far in the clouds
that one day you'll be struck by lightning!
You're eleven now, Belle, and should be
more responsible." Her mother shook her
head.

"Actually, it was a bird in the tree," Belle
mumbled, looking down at her basket of
eggs. "I'll wash these right away." She could
feel her mother staring as she busied herself
gently scrubbing the dirty eggs. This was
the third time this week her mother had

caught her daydreaming. If she didn't con-
centrate on her chores, she was going to get
into big trouble. She wished she could stop,
but the warm sun and the chirping birds
always put her in a mind to sing.

She picked up an egg and inspected it.
She loved to sing and she was good at it.
A happy little tune she'd heard at school
bubbled up through her brain. She began
humming cheerfully as she worked.

One day she would go to the big opera
houses in Montreal and perform for thou-
sands of people, who would clap and stamp
their feet, yelling for more! She could see
it all now. There would be loud cheering
and...*Crack*! The egg she was washing
broke and a splat of gooey yellow yolk slid
into the sink.

"Non, non, non, child!" her mother scolded.
"What am I going to do with you? I need
every one of those eggs. Monsieurs Louis
Riel and Gabrielle Dumont are coming
tonight and they will want to eat before the
meeting."

"Another meeting! Oh Mama, that means
the men will be up talking until very late."

4

Belle would get little sleep with all the noisy discussions about the troubles. The troubles, her brother Patrice said, had to do with the Canadian government trying to take their land away. The Metis people could not allow that.

Belle and her family were Metis—a blend of European and First Nations' people. Her great-grandfather, a white man, had come to this country from France and married her great-grandmother, a Cree lady. Their children were the first Metis in their family. Belle thought she was very Canadian because the Metis had begun here in Canada.

Nearly all the people of Batoche were Metis and supported Monsieur Riel. In 1870, he'd won a battle with the Canadian government at the Red River settlement. Everyone was hoping he could do it again now in 1885 here in Batoche. Belle's father and brother, who made their living hauling freight with the big, two-wheeled wooden Red River carts, were sure Monsieur Riel would make the Canadian government listen to the Metis people.

"Do I have to candle them?" Belle asked, looking at the row of gleaming white eggs on the counter. She disliked that job as she often missed the telltale dark spot on the inside of the egg when she held it up to the candle's light.

"Non, I have an errand for you. I want you to take this note to Father Moulin." Her mother handed Belle a slip of paper. "And try not to be too long."

Belle grinned. "Is this about who will be chosen as the new bell ringer at the church?" she asked, dancing from one foot to the other.

"Oui, Father Moulin will appoint the bell ringer on Sunday. I have heard that only one young person has asked for the job and I want to assure him that you are still very interested." She smiled at her daughter. "Am I wrong, ma petite fille?" Her mother tucked an errant strand of hair behind Belle's ear.

"Oh no, Mama!" Belle shook her head, releasing the strand of hair to fly free once more. "I still want to be the one to make Marie-Antoinette sing!" She stuffed the note into her apron pocket and raced out the door.

Bishop Grandin had presented their new church, St. Antoine de Padoue, with the bell last year when construction had finished. It had cost twenty-five dollars and was made of real silver! The bell had been christened Marie-Antoinette. She had a beautiful voice. Early every Sunday morning, she could be heard calling everyone to mass. To be the bell ringer would be a very important job, so important the person appointed was to have their name and picture printed in the paper!

Belle didn't care about the paper; she wanted to be the one to set Marie-Antoinette's voice free every Sunday. Her stomach fluttered. To be the bell ringer at St. Antoine de Padoue would be the most wonderful job in the world!

Belle sang in the church choir and had been told she had the best voice of all the children. She had often sung the exact same note the bell was chiming as she walked to church. Why, she and Marie-Antoinette already sang together every Sunday. It made Belle feel very special.

Belle rounded the corner of Monsieur Letendre's dry goods store and ran smack into Sarah Johnson. Belle and Sarah had never seen eye to eye on anything.

Sarah was Belle's age. She had moved to Batoche earlier that year from Fort Carlton. Her family was not Metis. They were very wealthy and had built a large house near the ferry crossing.

Sarah always wore beautiful clothes, all new and made by a factory in the east. She even had a petticoat that made her dress rustle when she walked! She was also very pretty, which she never let anyone forget. Even at school, she wore her pale blonde hair combed in an elaborate style and tiny gold earrings on her ears.

When they'd first met, Belle had tried to be friends with her, but Sarah disliked getting dirty or playing with anyone she called "riff raff." Belle had decided she must be riff raff, because Sarah never wanted to play with her. The other children at school said Sarah was so stuck-up that "her nose hid the sun." Belle liked Sarah's five-year-old brother Samuel who was not stuck-up at all. He was always smiling even when his mama dressed him in silly short pants.

"Look out, you clumsy girl!" Sarah exclaimed, a frown creasing her pretty forehead. "You should watch where you're going, Belle Tourond! You could have damaged my new hat!" She dusted off the bright blue hatbox she was carrying. "My mother ordered it for me all the way from Regina, and I don't want it ruined before Sunday."

Ignoring Sarah's rude comment, Belle stared at the box with new respect. A hat all the way from Regina! Unbelievable! "Can I see it?" she asked, her voice a reverent whisper. "I've never worn a real hat to mass before, just the scarf I got for Christmas three years ago."

Sarah hesitated, as though weighing whether or not Belle deserved the honor. Then she carefully lifted the lid off the round box. Inside, nestled in crisp white tissue paper, was the most beautiful hat Belle had ever seen. It was made of pale pink velvet and had an honest to good-ness feather sticking out of the side.

The feather exactly matched the velvet hat. What magical bird had produced such a feather?

"It's wonderful!" Belle breathed. She reached out a finger to stroke the delicate pink feather, but Sarah snatched the hatbox away.

"Don't touch!" she cried, replacing the lid. "You'll get it dirty." She grinned slyly at Belle. "I shall wear it to church on Sunday when Father Moulin announces that I will be the new bell ringer. I want to look good for my picture."

Belle's mouth dropped open.

2

Stepping in It

The next day at school, Belle was still thinking about Sarah's announcement. The rude blonde girl had no business wanting the job of bell ringer! After all, Sarah and her family were new to Batoche. They had no roots here as Belle's family did.

"Did you hear?" Bertha Lange asked as soon as they'd taken their seats. Bertha sat in front of Belle and had masses of carrot-colored hair that stuck out from her head like an orange haystack. The unruly mop often blocked Belle's view of the small blackboard at the front of the classroom.

"Hear what?" Belle asked, already knowing the answer.

"Sarah Johnson wants the job of bell ringer at the church!" Bertha's face was red with excitement. Sarah was Bertha's ideal of a perfect lady.

Belle looked to where Sarah sat giggling as she showed two boys her new black patent leather shoes. They must have come in yesterday with the hat, Belle decided. She looked down at her own scuffed brown shoes. Although they were hand-me-downs from her cousin who'd never been careful with her things, they were still much more suitable for playing in than those glossy dancing slippers Sarah had on.

Sarah looked over at Belle, made a face, then bent over and dusted off the shiny shoes before taking her seat.

Miss Onesime Dorval, their teacher, who was also the choir director at church, tapped her ruler on the desk. She taught all the grades in their one-room school and was very old and very strict. "Today we're going to read one of my favorite poems by a gentleman called Mr. William Wordsworth. It is entitled *I Wandered*

Lonely as a Cloud. Bertha, please hand these out." She pointed to a pile of papers with her ruler.

While the pages were being distributed, Miss Dorval scanned the room, a scowl creasing her already wrinkled forehead. Then her gaze fell on Sarah and one corner of her mouth twitched into what passed for a smile.

Belle groaned inwardly. Sarah was Miss Dorval's pet.

The teacher nodded at her favorite student. "Sarah Johnson, please read the opening stanza."

Sarah, her blonde curls bouncing, stood and walked with exaggerated steps to the front of the room, drawing as much attention as possible to her new shoes.

She cleared her throat loudly. "I wandered lonely as a cloud that floats on high o'er vales and hills. When all at once I saw a crowd, A host of golden daffodils..."

Belle glanced out the window and was surprised to see Daisy, Madame Carriere's cow, eating the flowers out of the Garnot's yard. What flavor would the milk be after the cow had eaten all the bright red tulips, she wondered.

"Belle Tourond!" Miss Dorval's stern voice made Belle jump.

Sarah, enjoying the spotlight, had almost finished the poem before Miss Dorval got her stopped. "Thank you, Sarah. Beautifully done. You may take your seat," she said, bestowing a warm smile on the beaming Sarah.

She turned to Belle. "Since we were all paying attention and following along on our sheets, I know you will be able to finish reading the poem for the class."

Belle looked down at her paper. Her reading skills weren't the best and she had no idea where Sarah had stopped. She swallowed as she scanned the poem trying to figure out where to start. Hadn't she heard Sarah say something about money or ... wealth! That was it, the second to last stanza talked about wealth.

Belle took a deep breath and read the last verse of the poem. "And then my heart with pleasure fills, And dances with the daffodils." She sat down. It really was an interesting poem. Sometimes words made pictures in your head and this poem, with its beautiful description of the bright yellow flowers, made wonderful images appear in Belle's mind.

"Sarah, would you please explain to the class what wealth Mr. Wordsworth was talking about in this great poem." Miss Dorval picked up her chalk and stood waiting beside the blackboard.

Sarah shuffled through the pages several times as though looking for the answer hidden on one of them, then slowly stood. "Oh, well, of course, Miss Dorval. Mr. William Wordsworth was talking about flowers…daffodils." She paused and swallowed. "And how he could pick them to sell at the local store to make money."

Belle snorted and Miss Dorval glared at her. "That's not quite right, Sarah, but a wonderful try. Belle, what do you think the reference to wealth means?" The scowling teacher folded her arms and waited.

Belle looked down at the paper. The other students giggled. "I think he's saying he didn't realize it when he was watching them

15

down by the shore, but the best thing the flowers did for him was to make a picture in his head that he could conjure up anytime he wanted."

Miss Dorval stared at her for a moment. "Actually…actually, you're correct." She looked like she hated saying it. "The wealth the flowers gave him was the recurring pleasure the memory of the dancing daffodils was able to provide."

Sarah glared at Belle from her seat at the front of the room.

Belle stuck her tongue out and crossed her eyes at Sarah. She might not be able to read as quickly as Miss Perfect Sarah, but somehow when she read the meaning of the words came into her head all the same. Belle liked books. Heck, reading one could take her an entire month! And her mother never interrupted her when she was doing important stuff like reading, which meant sometimes she could put off doing her chores for a little longer.

When Belle left the classroom after school, all the kids were gathered around the steps of the schoolhouse listening to

Sarah talk about being named the new bell ringer.

"...And as my family contributes so generously to the poor box, it is only fitting that I be named the official bell ringer on Sunday." She looked at her crowd of admirers as though daring them to disagree.

"Belle Tourond wants the job too, but her family can't possibly give as much to the church as yours does, Sarah," Bertha Lange gushed in a flowery voice that made Belle want to gag.

The gauntlet had been thrown down. Everyone turned to stare at Belle. She had no choice but to defend her family's honor.

"That's true, but my family does other things for the church. Last fall, my father and brother reshingled the roof so we wouldn't be leaked on for the Christmas pageant." Everyone murmured agreement with Belle.

Sarah came back, both guns blazing. "So what? When we moved here, my mother donated two silver candlesticks for the altar. Real ones, from England," she added, pointing to the east as though she could

17

see the store where the candlesticks had been bought. The crowd, nodding their heads, jumped back onto Sarah's side.

Belle pursed her lips trying to think of something to top the silver candlesticks, something that would stop Sarah in her tracks. Then she remembered a very important fact that no one had mentioned. "Hey Sarah. Aren't you forgetting something about the person who will be named the bell ringer? Something that has nothing to do with money?"

Everyone turned to Sarah. A hush fell over the crowd. This was unexpected. Sarah was silent, waiting to hear what could possibly be more important than money.

Belle screwed up her face in concentration. "If I remember correctly, the person named to be the official bell ringer is going to be chosen from the church choir. Last time I was at practice, I don't remember seeing you there." This was true. Father Moulin had clearly said only choir members were being considered for the important job. She smiled sweetly at Sarah whose face was now an ugly shade of red with purple blotches on her neck.

Sarah's eyes narrowed. "Oh really?" she hissed. "Well, I will be by Sunday! And I'm going to win this contest, so there!"

Belle glanced beyond Sarah to the dirt path that ran in front of the school. From the evidence left behind, she now knew where Madame Carriere's cow had gone after it had eaten the tulips.

Before Belle could warn her, Sarah turned with a whirl that made her full skirt flare out around her and stepped onto the path. There was a wet squishing sound, then a gasp from Bertha.

Looking down at her shoes, which were now covered with fresh cow manure, Sarah let out a wail that could be heard all the way to Regina. The other children laughed and pointed at the disgusting mess on Sarah's patent leather shoes, no longer so new or so shiny.

As Miss Dorval rushed out of the schoolhouse to see what the noise was about, Belle stuck her hands in her pockets, strolled past the shrieking Sarah and headed for home. No matter what, she was not going to let Sarah beat her.

3

Beautiful Bells and Stinky Smells

That night, Belle had to be told three times to bring hot water from the stove for the dishes. Finally, her mother put her hands on her hips and gave her daughter a knowing look.

"What is it, ma petite Belle? You don't seem very interested in getting these dishes clean."

Belle looked at her mother, not wanting to tell her about Sarah, but finally relenting. "Someone else wants the job of bell ringer." She poured hot water from a bucket onto the waiting dishes in the sink. Clouds of steam rose, blurring her vision.

"Oh really! Who?" her mother asked, scrubbing at the dishes, her hands turning red in the hot water.

"Sarah Johnson." Belle tried to sound calm, but her mother gave her a sidelong glance.

"And this has you worried? Belle, you have the best voice in the choir and have been going to this church since you were born. Father Moulin will make the right choice. He's a fair man."

Belle smiled. "And Sarah isn't even a member of the choir, which is one of the rules." Her mother was right. Of course, she would be chosen. As fragrant coffee brewed on the stove, they finished the dishes in silence.

Belle helped her mother take the coffee, cups, milk and sugar into the living room where her father and Patrice were visiting with Jean Caron. Monsieur Caron had been one of the first settlers in the Batoche area and his son Pierre went to school with Belle. Pierre also sang in the choir at church.

"Monsieur Riel has sent a petition to Prime Minister Macdonald with our demands, but nothing is happening," Monsieur Caron was saying when Belle returned with a plate of freshly baked bannock and Saskatoon preserves.

"They want to survey our land in the English way, so that we will not have access to the river. Impossible! We also want representation in the Canadian Parliament, which the government won't give us." Belle had heard these arguments before. She knew they were serious matters.

"And don't forget the government wants to tax us too!" Patrice added, reaching for a piece of bannock.

"After the battle at Duck Lake, they will not listen to us," her father said. "Lives have been lost on both sides, but the English will only remember their own dead."

Patrice put his cup down so hard some spilt over the edge into the saucer. "Then perhaps Monsieur Riel is right. We Metis should break away from Canada and form our own country where we can live in peace."

Belle's mother motioned for her to leave and, reluctantly, she started up the stairs to bed. Sometimes when the men talked, she got a tight knot in her stomach. She tried not to be afraid, but all the adults talked about lately were the troubles and how things were getting worse.

Early Sunday morning, Marie-Antoinette's clear voice called the people of Batoche to mass at St. Antoine de Padoue church.

Belle had taken special care with her braids this morning. She had even tried to shine her scuffed shoes. She'd put on her best green dress, the one her mother had embroidered with beautiful flowers so that it looked like a piece of a summer meadow had come to life.

She was excited as she sat in the pews at the side of the altar with the rest of the choir. Her parents and brother were in their usual seats. Her mother looked lovely in her black hat and Sunday dress and her father was positively handsome in his Sunday suit. Belle felt a surge of love for her parents.

She glanced at the rest of the children in the two choir pews. They didn't seem to be the least bit excited. But then, she thought, they weren't going to be named the new bell ringer.

Miss Dorval walked over and called them to attention by tapping her ever-present ruler on the front railing of the pew. "Children, I have an announcement which I know you will all be very happy about." Unease mixed with Belle's excitement. "I am pleased to introduce to you our newest choir member, Miss Sarah Johnson." She nodded toward the congregation and Sarah, who had been sitting with her parents, stood up and marched over. She looked very pretty in her expensive gray wool coat with pink trim and she was wearing her new hat with the magical feather.

Shooting a triumphant grin at Belle, Sarah took a seat beside Pierre Caron, who was by himself in the front choir pew.

Belle's temper flared before she remembered where she was. This was a church, not the place to think bad thoughts. Instead, Belle turned to her hymnbook and smiled. Beside her, Marie Savant, who had a beautiful voice, nudged Belle with her elbow and giggled. Belle's smile widened just a little.

Pierre Caron was a nice enough fellow, but he was not a favorite of the other choir singers. He was nicknamed Windy Caron. Pierre had a digestion problem that made him not only noisy to stand beside, but impossible to breathe around. When Windy got wound up, no one could sing beside him.

The congregation rose as Father Moulin entered. There was a muffled rumble from the front pew. Sarah made a choking sound, then glared at Pierre, her hand flying to her nose.

"Before we get started today, mes amis, I have an announcement." Father Moulin walked over to stand beside the choir. "As you know, we have been searching for a young person to be the official bell ringer here at St. Antoine de Padoue." He smiled at the young singers. "We decided it was only fitting that this person should be chosen from the choir as Marie-Antoinette loves to sing as much as these children."

Sarah tried to ease her way down the pew away from Windy, who had bragged to the rest of them that he'd feasted on fourteen pickled pigs' feet last night and that his stomach didn't feel very good. Unfortunately for Sarah, the spare hymnbooks were piled in the pew beside her. She had nowhere to go.

"Until this week, my choice was easy. Only one brave soul wanted the job." He smiled at Belle. "But as of this morning, we have two willing volunteers: Belle Tourond and Sarah Johnson." The congregation murmured. "Choosing a winner is no easy task, but..." He paused, and Belle held her breath. "To be fair to both young ladies, I have decided to hold a contest. Miss Dorval suggested that each girl embroider a cloth suitable to adorn the altar. The girl whose work is judged the best will be our new bell ringer. Miss Dorval and I will decide on the winner two weeks from today, on May third. Good luck to both young ladies."

Sarah, still not able to breathe easily, made a face that was as sour as Pierre's stomach.

Belle tried to look confident, but her heart was sinking fast. She could sing very well, but learning embroidery had never appealed to her.

4

Perfect Stitches and Hidden Ditches

Belle went to work. Why should she worry about Sarah when her own mother was the world's best when it came to fancy stitching? Hadn't she embroidered the tiny flowers on Belle's beautiful Sunday dress and didn't she sew all their clothes by hand?

Belle listened while her mother explained how to do various stitches and then she practiced on an old pillowcase while her mother looked for a suitable piece of material for the altar cloth.

"I know just what design I want to create," Belle announced to her mother as she finished a rather lopsided French knot. "It will be a colorful pattern of prairie wildflowers with big black-eyed Susans, bright blue harebells and pale pink wild roses and happy yellow buffalo beans in a field of brilliant green sweetgrass covering the entire cloth."

Her mother raised an eyebrow. "My, that is ambitious!" She looked thoughtful for a moment. "Perhaps a border of sweetgrass with the flowers twined together at the four corners of the cloth would be better, Belle. Embroidery done correctly takes many hours and I know you want to finish in time." She held up a long rectangle of snow-white linen. "This was a wedding present from your grandmother. I've been saving it for something special."

Belle's eyes went wide as she reached out to touch the cloth. "It's perfect," she whispered, then she realized how much sewing it would take to cover the entire cloth with her flower design. "On second thought, perhaps you're right. A wonderful flower border would be most suitable for the altar cloth." She ran to her workbook and ripped out a clean piece of paper. On this, she carefully drew the design she had in mind, and her mother suggested which stitches would work best.

"I think this outline stitch will help you make the flower patterns and you can use the satin stitch to fill in the petals." Her mother showed Belle how to sew the stitches on the old pillowcase. Her fingers flew, and before Belle's amazed eyes a flower pattern took shape. "To finish, I think we should use the whipped stem stitch on the flowers to give the design more depth." With a few deft strokes, the flower came to life and turned into a daisy.

"Do you really think I can do this Mama?" Belle touched the flower with her fingertip.

Her mother laughed. "Of course you can! You just need to practice." She gave Belle a quick squeeze. "I think you will do a wonderful job."

Belle was filled with confidence. She went over and over the complicated stitches needed to create the lovely effects for her masterpiece. Painstakingly, she sewed and re-sewed fern, satin and chain stitches as well as the fly stitch, which her mother thought would look good on the border as a background for the flowers.

Finally, she felt ready to start sewing on the beautiful piece of material that her mother had given her.

Belle tried to be careful as she stitched the first flower on the cloth. But when she looked at it with a critical eye, it was not at all what she'd imagined. With a sigh, she picked out the stitches and started over. It had to be perfect.

Belle worked and reworked the stitching until she was satisfied it was as good as she could make it, but every night when she put the cloth away, she wished she'd done an even better job.

"I think it looks wonderful, Belle," her mother said one evening when she checked on the progress of the cloth.

Belle felt a little better, but she still worried the cloth wasn't perfect enough to guarantee that she would win.

While working on her sewing, Belle noticed her father also looked worried, but she knew it had nothing to do with embroidery. News had come from Fish Creek that on April 24th there had been a big battle between the Metis and a General Middleton who was in command of the government forces. It had been a victory for the Metis, but reports of new battles were coming more and more often, and Belle wondered what was going to happen. It had been reported that five thousand government troops were coming on the new Canadian Pacific Railway to help in the fight against the Metis. This seemed strange to Belle because her papa said they had only three hundred Metis who could fight.

Monsieur Dumont had the men setting up defenses and digging fortifications called rifle pits in case they were attacked. Everyone hoped the pits wouldn't be needed, but they kept digging them anyway.

When Belle was walking home one day, she noticed that several of the earthwork pits had been dug along the edge of the cemetery. She shivered. The large open holes so close to the graves filled her with foreboding. They were so well hidden that you would never see anyone crouching there until it was too late.

Belle walked on past the church and onto Jolie Prairie, the wide-open expanse of grassland where the Humboldt Trail crossed the trail to St. Laurent. The air was chilly and she wondered if real spring was ever going to come. The gray poplars and leafless willows reached out from the dead prairie grass as though pleading with the sun to share more of her warmth. A soft breeze had sprung up and it sounded like the world was sadly sighing.

Belle turned toward home on the outskirts of Batoche away from all the other houses. She loved where her parents had built their home. It was on a slight rise. You could see down across the town and all the shops on the main street to where the ferryboat crossed the big river. On summer evenings, when the sun was disappearing into the green sea of grass far in the distance, the town looked as if it were made of rose-colored buildings surrounded by motes of golden dust. The grasshoppers would be chirping as Belle sat on her porch steps breathing in the fragrant evening air.

Today, as she started along the edge of the ridge she noticed something strange about the embankment beneath her feet. Wooden boards ran along the edge of the cliff and what looked to be an old door was set into the side of the hill. It was nearly covered with old grass and leaves. Belle would never have seen it if she hadn't decided to cut across the slope to save time. She was supposed to be home doing her embroidery, not tramping around looking for hidden rifle pits.

Investigating further, she discovered a handle on the weathered door and pulled. It groaned and creaked, then something splintered and the heavy door opened a little. Belle peered into the darkness inside. The air was musty and smelled of mould and damp earth. It was an abandoned root cellar where vegetables would have been stored to keep them through the winter.

Belle carefully lowered the weathered door. She put her hands on her hips. How about that! All the years she'd lived here and she'd never noticed this old root cellar before. It was so overgrown with grasses and Saskatoon bushes that no one would have known it was here.

The whistle from the five o'clock ferryboat made Belle jump. How could it be so late? She'd let time slip away again! She had no excuses left. All thoughts of the old cellar flew out of her head as she hiked up her skirt and ran for home.

5

Butter Papers and Soapsuds

Belle stayed up late into the night, sometimes until ten o'clock, working on her
embroidery. The design was slowly taking
shape. It even looked like she'd imagined, if
you ignored the places where she'd torn out
the stitches so many times that the material was a little stretched. She had one more
flower and a corner piece of the border to
do before the beautiful cloth would be finished. There were two days left and Belle
was sure she could do it. Sunday was going
to be a day she would always remember.

"Belle!" her mother called from the back
porch. "Come here, please. I need you to
run an errand for me."

Frowning, Belle looked down at the cloth.

She was starting the last bright buffalo bean, and wanted to make sure she had the shape of the delicate yellow flower just right. Maybe she could pretend she hadn't heard her mama call...

"Now, Belle, s'il vous plait!"

Belle sighed. She placed the cloth on the sideboard and hurried to see what her mother wanted.

"There you are." Her mother was working the butter churn. One bowl of fresh, sweet butter was already sitting on the table. She stopped and drew a coin from the pocket of her skirt. "I want you to run to Monsieur Letendre's store and bring me back a dozen butter papers. And please don't dawdle."

Belle started for the store. The butter was wrapped in greased butter papers before it was placed in the icehouse. Belle loved fresh butter and knew the papers helped keep it from spoiling. It was a wonderful day for a walk. She turned down Main Street where Monsieur Letendre's store stood tall and imposing in the afternoon sunshine.

Her hand tightened on the coin in her pocket as she pushed the door open and entered the cool dark interior. The shop not only had food stocked on shelves and in baskets along one wall, but it also carried bolts of cloth and saddles, not to mention bottles of patent medicine and tobacco.

Belle's favorite thing in the store was the wheel of cheese as big around as her arms could reach. It sat on top of a barrel beside the counter where the ornate brass cash register rang up the sales. Monsieur Letendre cut off a sliver of cheese for each young person who came by, asking them to give their opinion as to the quality and flavor. He listened to the children's opinions with a serious expression. It was the most delicious cheese Belle had ever tasted.

Glancing around the store, Belle was surprised to see an old woman with a black shawl around her head standing at the front counter paying for her purchases.

Madame Coteau was as old as sod and had a reputation as being a shaman or wise woman. Most of the children called her a witch and no one dared to go near her house. She had treated many sick people and healed those whom the travelling doctor couldn't help. But some said that healing wasn't all she did. It was whispered that perfectly healthy people became ill after running afoul of Madame Coteau. She lived alone on the far side of the river and Belle had not seen her since last fall, before the snows.

Old Madame Coteau wasn't the only person standing at the counter. Sarah Johnson was also there with a basket full of potatoes and onions. Belle walked up to the counter and stood waiting. Monsieur Letendre kept the butter papers on the shelf behind the till, so she would have to ask him for them. Madame Coteau paid for her purchases and left as Sarah pushed her basket of vegetables toward the shop-keeper. "Charge these to my parents' bill."

Monsieur Letendre glanced up and saw Belle waiting. "I'll be with you in a moment, Belle." Then a twinkle came into his eye. "Say, aren't you both in the contest over at the church? How's that coming along, ladies?"

"My cloth is finished and it's absolute-ly marvelous!" Sarah gushed, not giving

Belle time to speak. "I can hardly wait for Sunday! It will be such an honor to have my altar cloth chosen." She looked at Belle out of the corner of her eye. "And to be the only one who will get to ring Marie-Antoinette every Sunday morning!" She emphasized "the only one," in case Belle hadn't figured that part out.

Monsieur Letendre put the potatoes in the scale, walked to the end of the counter and cut a generous slice of cheese, which he handed to Belle. "And how is yours coming along, mon petite?" He cut a smaller sliver and offered it to Sarah before going back to the weigh scale.

Belle smiled. "My cloth is also finished, and it has turned out very nicely. Thank you for asking." This wasn't completely true, but it was close enough that Belle didn't think of it as even a little white lie. She took a big bite of her cheese slice, relishing the crumbly texture and strong flavor of the aged cheddar.

"You children are too young to remember, but that elderly woman who was just in here could have taught you both a thing or two about needlework. Why, Agnes Coteau could sew circles around any gal in the territory. She won more prizes at the annual fair than you could shake a stick at." He handed Sarah a paper sack with her vegetables and jotted down an amount in his accounts ledger. "The only lady who even came close was your own mother, Belle. Your ma could take a plain coat and turn it into a work of art, and as for weaving, well, half the Metis in Batoche are wearing sashes your mother made."

Belle knew her mother was very good at sewing, but she didn't realize that her weaving skills were so well known. She was teaching Belle how to make the colorful Red River or L'Assumption sash which was the traditional woven belt that Metis wore around their waists. Belle's smile widened as she felt a surge of pride for her mother and a new interest in her own weaving. Sarah ignored the flowery compliments. She tilted her face up until she was looking down her nose at Belle and the shopkeeper. "My own family simply purchases any items they need. It has always been felt that a real lady shouldn't bother herself with such boring tasks as sewing." And with that, she spun around and flounced out of the store.

"That girl has a lot of growing up to do, I reckon." Monsieur Letendre shook his head and turned back to Belle. "Now, young lady, what can I do for you?"

Belle was still thinking about what Sarah had said. She felt a little wave of self-doubt when she remembered how confident Sarah had sounded. What if Sarah's cloth was better? What if Belle wasn't the one who released Marie-Antoinette's silvery voice every Sunday morning? Everyone knew it was Belle's mother who was famous for her needlework, not Belle. Her mother had been very firm about not sewing one stitch on the precious cloth. She'd said it wouldn't be fair if she did more than show Belle how to do the stitches. It must be Belle who did all the embroidery.

Belle's eye fell on a bright blue box sitting on the shelf behind Monsieur Letendre. It read, "Snow White Soap Flakes, Clothes so snowy white, your neighbors will talk!"

"I'll take the box of Snow White Soap Flakes, please." She laid the money for the butter papers on the counter. Belle was sure her mother would understand when she saw the box of washing powder. After all, what mother wouldn't want her daughter to have an altar cloth so snowy white that people talked!

6

Judgement Day

Belle had to do some very inventive talking when she arrived home without the butter papers, but in the end, her mother understood.

"I suppose I would have done the same thing," she said. "I think you should finish the cloth so we can try out your new soap powder. I wouldn't want to keep all the neighbors waiting."

Belle hugged her mother. "Thank you, Mama. I promise, I will do extra chores to pay for the soap."

Her mother laughed. "I would settle for you doing your regular chores on time!"

Belle worked hard on finishing her beautiful cloth, checking to make sure every flower was exactly right when seen from what she thought was an appropriate distance. She would stand across the room and pretend she was sitting in the front pew of the church. Then she would peer at her cloth as though seeing it for the first time. It looked perfect. She smiled to herself. In fact, it looked even more perfect the farther away you were!

Satisfied, Belle decided her first embroidery project was done and just in time. Tomorrow, at mass, the winner would be announced.

"Look, Mama, it's done! What do you think?" Belle said as she held the cloth up for her mother's inspection. "I can wash it now"

Her mother viewed the cloth with a critical eye. "No one would know this is your first time embroidering. It's lovely, Belle. You did a wonderful job!"

Belle glowed under her mother's praise. "I'll heat the water to give it a bath." She giggled. "I mean a bubble bath!"

Not sure how much of the Snowy White Soap Flakes to put in the water, Belle poured a generous portion into the steaming tub. Swirling the water around to melt the flakes, she was amazed at how the lather first expanded, then overflowed the washtub. There were soapsuds everywhere! Belle washed the cloth carefully, making sure all her dirty fingerprints were scrubbed away.

When it came time to rinse the cloth, getting rid of the excess bubbles proved a tougher job than Belle would have expected. The more she sloshed the water around to rinse them away, the more suds formed. It took her longer to get rid of all the lather than it had to go to the store and buy the soap powder in the first place!

Finally, all the bubbles were gone and the cloth rinsed. Carefully, she hung the gleaming white work of art to dry. Tomorrow she would have to get up early to light the stove so the flat iron needed to press the cloth could be heated. She didn't want one wrinkle to detract from the pretty pattern of flowers and grass.

Early the next morning, Belle dressed in her best outfit. She even mended the small tear in her scarf that she wore to mass. Her family laughed at how nervous she was.

"You would think the queen of England was coming today. All this fuss, mon dieu!" Patrice teased Belle, but he put on a clean shirt and slicked his hair down neatly anyway.

At church, Belle placed her cloth next to Sarah's on the table at the front then took her place with the rest of the choir. The other children spread out in the pew so that Sarah was forced to sit beside Windy Caron again. This time Sarah built a protective wall of hymnals between her and her fragrant choir mate.

When Father Moulin entered, the children stood and began to sing. Sarah, who had attended only one practice since joining the choir, fumbled with her hymnbook trying to find the right song.

"Come over here and you can use my book," Windy Caron offered with a toothy grin. "We had cabbage rolls for supper last night!"

Sarah glared at him and began pretending to sing, while still frantically looking for the right page in her book.

Belle could hardly sit through the sermon. The winner would be announced at the end of mass. She kept looking over at the two embroidered cloths. She had to admit Sarah's did look nice. The design was a cleverly worked dove holding an olive branch in its mouth as it soared in a pale blue sky. The stitching around the edge was a complicated pattern that showed off Sarah's obvious needle skills. Belle tried not to be jealous. Hers was still beautiful with all the carefully worked flowers, but it wasn't as showy as Sarah's intricate pattern.

Finally, the service ended. "I have an announcement!" Father Moulin called. "I wish to draw your attention to these fine examples of needlework by two of our young people." He nodded to the choir mistress to leave her seat and approach the table. "Miss Dorval and myself will choose one of these cloths as the winner of our contest and that young lady will be our new bell ringer."

Belle held her breath as the two judges inspected the cloths. Sarah smiled smugly. Her confidence didn't help Belle's nervousness.

Miss Dorval took out her spectacles and perched them on the bridge of her nose. She inspected each piece for a long time. Then, without warning, the choir mistress did an unexpected thing. She turned the cloths over and looked at the other side of the work!

Belle cringed as she saw the tangle of threads and loose ends adorning the back of her cloth. Sarah's was as neat on the back as it was decorative on the front. Belle had no idea that side of the cloth would be looked at. She groaned inwardly.

The two judges conferred. Then Father Moulin faced the congregation. "Both cloths are truly remarkable. We would be honored to use either on the altar at St. Antoine de Padoue and we hope both cloths will be donated to the church." He turned to the choir where Belle and Sarah waited. "We have decided to award the honor of bell ringer to…"

Belle held her breath.

"... Miss Sarah Johnson!"

The congregation murmured and a couple of loud grumbles of disagreement could be heard from friends of the Tourond family. The Johnsons clapped loudly, but no one else joined in. Clearly, Sarah was not the crowd favorite.

Sarah walked to the table, the pink feather in her hat bobbing gaily as she went. The newspaper reporter waited at the front of the church with his cumbersome equipment. The cloth-draped camera box was supported on a tripod, and the gentleman held a flashpan high over his head. He would ignite this to produce light for Sarah's all-important picture.

Belle watched the production in stunned silence. She gulped, trying not to show her disappointment. It was going to be hard to walk to church now. To her, Marie-Antoinette's clear silvery voice would sound sad.

7

Suspicious Kindness

"The government troops have a nine-pound cannon and a new type of gun that shoots many rounds per minute. It's called a Gatling gun, and we have nothing to match it." Patrice reached for more tea, but the pot was empty. Belle's mother whisked the teapot off to the kitchen.

It was Wednesday evening and there was another meeting at Belle's house. She couldn't help but overhear the adults' conversation as she busily mended her papa's shirt. Now that she was such an experienced needle worker, her mother said she should not let her skills get rusty. Mending the family's clothes was one way to stay sharp.

Sitting quietly in the corner, Belle tried not to worry at every new revelation she heard.

"We've sent word to Poundmaker, Big Bear and the Blackfoot to join with us." Belle's father lit his old pipe, puffing until the smoke curled up around his head.

Belle loved the smell of her father's pipe tobacco. The sweet smoky scent meant home to her. By listening quietly, she had found out the reason there were so many meetings at her house: Monsieur Riel had appointed her father to his provisional government. This council would oversee the running of the new country, should the Metis have to break away from Canada.

Gabriel Dumont ran his hand through his long brown hair. "One thing is for certain: If we have to fight, we will need more ammunition."

Belle's mother returned with fresh tea. She set the teapot down and looked at it thoughtfully. "The women can help with that. We store our tea in lead chests. We will melt the tea chests down and make bullets."

Monsieur Dumont smiled at Belle's mother. "Tres bien, Madame Tourond. Make no mistake, it will come to that."

Belle thought of her mother's tea chest. It had been in her family for generations. The offer to melt it down meant only one thing. The Metis would fight with everything they had to defend themselves and their way of life.

At school Thursday, Belle was surprised at how few of her classmates mentioned seeing Sarah's picture in the newspaper. Bertha, of course, had a copy of the paper and pinned Sarah's picture up on the classroom wall. Sarah stood beside it as though it was the most important thing in the world.

In the playground after school, the children's talk was all about what they had heard from their parents concerning "the troubles." It seemed they were all a little frightened about what they had heard.

"My parents are thinking of sending me and my sister to stay with relatives in Winnipeg," Andrew Taggert said, nudging a stone with the toe of his boot.

"And mine are stocking up on provisions, in case the government troops attack," Jenny Dumphrey added as she kicked her legs out to make the swing she was perched on go higher.

"My papa thinks the Metis of Batoche are being silly," Sarah said, pinning one of her golden ringlets back into place. "My papa says they are just a bunch of blowhards and should listen to what Prime Minister Macdonald tells them. My papa says all this blustering makes the Metis look like hotheads and spoilt children who don't know when they've got it good."

Belle, who hadn't said anything up until now, decided enough was enough. "Sarah, I'm glad your papa has done such a thorough job of investigating why everyone is up in arms! I guess he's not worried about losing his land when the government re-surveys it and chops it up into square blocks for the new settlers from the east because that's what will happen, even if you aren't Metis!" She'd heard her brother speak of this and knew it was one of the real concerns Monsieur Riel had taken to the prime minister.

Sarah stopped for a minute, then her brow furrowed. "We already have access to the river, so what do we care!"

Keeping their river frontage was vital to the Metis because they had always used the rivers to move goods around. If they couldn't get to the rivers, with so few roads available, the Metis would not be able to take their furs to the Hudson's Bay trading post.

Bertha came to stand beside Sarah, her wild orange hair contrasting sharply with Sarah's perfect golden curls. "Come on, Sarah. I'll push you on the swings."

It would do no good to reason with Sarah. Belle shook her head, picked up her book bag and left. She was going to visit Monsieur Letendre's store on her way home. Her mother had given her a penny to buy a stick of barley sugar candy as a reward for almost winning the contest.

"Consider it a prize for second place," she'd said, giving Belle the money. Her mother knew how hard Belle had worked and that it had hurt not to win.

Belle had been thinking of the sweet candy all day. She walked a little faster, hoping Monsieur Letendre would let her pick her own piece. Some were just a little larger than others, and Belle had spotted a dandy the last time she'd been sent to the store.

"I'm sorry you didn't win the contest, Belle," Monsieur Letendre said the moment she walked into the large store.

"Me too!" she agreed, shrugging her shoulders. It was no use fussing about the decision. Sarah had beaten her fair and square. "Sarah did do a good job and who knew Father Moulin and Miss Dorval would look at the back of the cloth! I never bothered about that side at all. No one sees it but God, and since he's getting both cloths for free, I didn't think he'd care if mine was a little messy!"

Monsieur Letendre laughed out loud, a big jolly laugh that made Belle giggle.

"I'd like to purchase a piece of your best barley sugar candy please." She put the penny on the counter. "And if it's all right with you, can I pick the piece I want?"

She hoped the bigger than average stick was still waiting for her.

The shopkeeper took the jar down from the shelf and put it on the counter in front of Belle. "Help yourself, mon ami!"

Inspecting the shiny candy, Belle searched for the special piece. "That one, s'il vous plait!" She pointed to a stick that was a fraction longer than all the rest.

Monsieur Letendre removed the piece of candy and handed it to Belle. Then he reached back into the jar and took out a second piece, tucking it into a small brown paper bag. "For later," he said, smiling as he handed her the bag.

Belle thanked him and took the extra treat. She smiled at the kind shopkeeper and was just about to leave when she happened to look across the street.

There, in the narrow lane between two stores, she saw something she didn't think she would ever see.

Sarah Johnson was talking to Madame Coteau! Then, as Belle watched, another unbelievable thing happened. Sarah handed the old woman money!

"Will you look at that!" Belle said in surprise. She knew that the old woman received help from the church's poor box to buy food and supplies.

Monsieur Letendre squinted as he peered across the street. "Maybe Miss Sarah's winning the contest has made her realize that she should help others less fortunate than herself."

Belle frowned. "It does look like that." She watched as the old woman put the money in her bag, then shuffled off down the alley.

Sarah skipped away without a backward glance.

Belle waved good-bye to the shopkeeper and started for home. She thought about what she'd seen. Maybe she had misjudged Sarah. Belle took another slow lick of the sweet barley candy. Perhaps Stuck-Up Sarah did have a little streak of kindness after all. But she didn't think so.

8

Setting a Trap to Catch the Truth

All the way home Belle puzzled over seeing Sarah and Madame Coteau together. It was very strange.

"Bonjour, Mama!" Belle called as she banged open the back door, but no one answered. A note told her to gather the eggs from the henhouse and peel a large pot of potatoes for supper. Belle blew on her sticky barley candy to dry it off. Then she put it into the paper bag with the second stick and tucked the bag in the cupboard.

Gathering eggs and peeling potatoes! She remembered her dream of singing in the big opera houses of Montreal and hummed as she headed out to the chicken coop.

As Belle rummaged around in the nest boxes, she thought about Sarah's odd act of kindness. "And for Miss Sarah, any act of kindness would be odd!" she told a hen as she pushed her off her nest to retrieve the warm prize.

Once she'd gathered the eggs, she sat down for a rest on the three-legged stool by the door to the henhouse. A hawk soared high above the brown prairie grass. The graceful bird circled, hovered and dove for an unfortunate field mouse. Again, Belle thought about the strange meeting she'd witnessed.

Madame Coteau had always been a mystery to the children of Batoche. She lived across the river in a broken down house that could only be described as spooky. No children ever went over there, at least none that returned to tell the tale!

Belle shivered in the waning afternoon sun. Although it was the first week of May, it was still unseasonably cool.

The back door slammed. There was her mother with her hands on her hips. The potatoes!

Belle jumped to her feet, grabbed the basket of eggs and raced for the house.

Her mother scolded her once again about having her head in the clouds.

"I'm sorry, Mama. I..."

But her mother didn't stop to hear Belle's latest excuse. Instead, she went to the potato bin and began pulling the vegetables out. "Never mind, never mind. I shouldn't have expected you to handle two chores in a row without supervision! One day, you will have no choice, Belle. People will be counting on you."

Usually Belle didn't pay much attention to her mother when she was scolded, but this time, the words her mother said stayed in her mind. A wave of guilt washed over her.

Belle hurried to wash the eggs so she could help her mother with the potatoes. As she finished peeling, she told her mama about the strange occurrence between Madame Coteau and Sarah.

"Perhaps she really has turned over a new leaf. Being the new bell ringer, maybe she decided to do a charitable act."

Her mother always could see the good side to everything.

"I think it's strange. Even if she is the new bell ringer, I don't think Sarah would turn over anything." As Belle worked on her potato, she noticed it shrank a lot as she sliced off large pieces of peel. An idea skittered around in her head, but it wouldn't sit still so she could get a good grasp on it.

They finished the peeling and Belle went to set the table. She was just getting the plates out of the sideboard when it hit her. She stopped halfway to the table with the dishes. Sarah was always talking about how she didn't do menial tasks like cleaning or cooking or sewing!

Here was a girl who didn't know how to thread a needle one week and won an embroidery contest the next! Belle supposed it could happen, but... She remembered Monsieur Letendre talking about what wonderful embroidery Madame Coteau used to do. Sarah was rich enough to hire someone to do anything she wanted—like embroider an altar cloth for the church!

What if Sarah had been paying Madame Coteau for embroidering the cloth for her? If Belle was right, Sarah would be disqualified and Belle would win the contest by default!

This was big news! But she had no proof. If she told Father Moulin or her mother what she suspected, they would think she was making the whole thing up out of jealousy.

No, she had to confront Sarah and find out if her suspicions were correct.

Friday morning began bright and sunny. Belle could hardly wait for class to be over for the day. She was going to corner Sarah and ask her who really sewed the cloth. The best place would be where there were witnesses, that way Belle would have others to back up her story.

When Sarah headed over to the teeter-totter, Belle knew her moment had come. Before Bertha could climb onto the empty side of the old painted board, Belle jumped on and moved as far out to the end as she could. She was heavier than Sarah and her sitting at the end made it sink to the ground. Sarah was suspended high in the air.

"What do you think you're doing, Belle? Let me down this minute!" Sarah kicked her feet and tried to bounce the board to the ground, but Belle hunkered down with all her weight.

"I've got a couple of questions for you, Sarah. Once you've answered them, I'll let you down, no problem." She squinted up at Sarah. The afternoon sun was directly behind her so that Belle couldn't see her face clearly.

"I saw you giving money to Madame Coteau. I think you were paying her for doing a favor for you, a very important favor." Belle waited for Sarah to deny paying the old lady. Then she'd have her. Belle had a witness; Monsieur Letendre had seen the whole thing too.

Sarah stopped thrashing her legs and peered down at Belle. "What do you mean, you saw me paying Madame Coteau yesterday?"

Others were gathering around now, sensing a potential fight.

Belle held on tight. She wasn't going to let Sarah off.

"I saw you giving her money and I think you were paying Madame Coteau for her embroidery skills. I think you had her sew that altar cloth and then you said it was your work!"

Sarah jerked her legs, trying to get her end of the board closer to the ground so she could jump off. "You're crazy, Belle Tourond! Yes, I saw the poor old lady yesterday. I felt so badly for her that I gave her my allowance to buy food." She made sure all their class-mates gathered around heard her. "How could you accuse me of cheating on the contest? You're a poor loser and are making up lies about me! Now, let me down!"

Belle knew she wasn't the one who was lying, but she hadn't expected Sarah to come up with such a good excuse for giving the old woman money. This girl was tricky! "Not until you admit you hired the old lady to embroider the cloth!" Belle thought about sliding off her end and letting Sarah drop to the ground, but decided that would be a little too much persuasion.

"I said let me down!" Sarah was screeching now, and the rest of the children on the playground were becoming excited.

"You'd better let my friend down if you know what's good for you!" Bertha Lange loomed over Belle. Her fists were balled up tight. She looked like a dog ready to bite!

Belle glanced up at Bertha, then back at Sarah, who was making pitiful sobbing noises. It was the phoniest crying Belle had ever heard. She looked back at Bertha. The girl's face was beet red and her eyeballs were bulging out of her head as if she were ready to explode.

Sliding forward, Belle lowered the protesting girl to the ground. Just before the teeter-totter touched down, she leapt off, making Sarah's landing a little harder than it might have been.

Sarah bumped to the ground and rolled off the painted plank. She struggled indignantly to her feet, readjusting her dress, which had flown up over her head with the impact of her abrupt stop.

"You'll be sorry for this, Belle Tourond. Just you wait! You're jealous because you lost the contest. Well, I won and I'm the new bell ringer and there's nothing you can do about it!" She spun around and stalked off, her pale blue dress a froth of ruffles and lace.

Belle thought she was walking a little stiffly, but a bump on the behind will do that to a person.

9

Belle's Plan

As she trudged home, Belle couldn't stop thinking about Sarah. She was sure she had cheated on the embroidery. Sarah hated anything to do with sewing; she only wanted to be the bell ringer to get her picture in the paper and maybe to show off her fancy hat.

Belle stopped to watch two men piling brush in front of one of the cleverly hidden rifle pits that now surrounded the town. For the last couple of days, all the adults had been rushing about doing grown-up things.

Perhaps Sarah had wanted to win just to show Belle, which would have been fine if Sarah had done it fairly. But Belle was sure she hadn't and to make matters worse, Sarah had lied in front of their classmates, making Belle look like a sore loser.

Sore loser, indeed! Belle had to get proof now. Her own reputation was at stake! But how could she do it? If Sarah had denied giving Madame Coteau money, Belle could have asked Monsieur Letendre to vouch for her story, but Sarah had been clever.

There was only one way to straighten the whole thing out. Belle would have to get proof. She would have to go to Madame Coteau!

Belle thought of the scary old woman. Stories of witches and evil shamans swirled in her mind. She put them out of her head. She had to go. It was the only way.

She hurried home. If she left right away, she could catch the last ferry over and back across the river.

"Mama, I need to go out for a while. I might not get back until after supper, but it's real important and I promise I'll do my chores when I get back." She hoped her mother wouldn't ask for more detail.

"No, my child. You can't go out. In fact,

you must stay in the house for the rest of the day." Her mother was bustling around the kitchen gathering preserves and dried meat.

This was unexpected. "But Mama, I will only be gone for a short time…" This was almost the truth, if you took out the time for the ferry crossings. After all, Belle had no control over how long the boat ride would take, so she shouldn't be held responsible for accounting for that time.

"You can't leave the house tonight!" Her mother's voice sounded worried.

"Mama, what has happened?" Then Belle saw the lead tea chest standing empty on the table. "Oh Mama! Are the Metis people going to war?" She was alarmed now.

Her mother stopped her rushing about and gave her daughter a hug. "Monsieur Riel says everything will be all right. We have God on our side. Do not worry, little one. Now, you must cook the meal tonight for your papa and brother. I am taking these provisions to the church and will be back later." She gathered the preserves and meat and placed them in an old sugar sack.

Then with a reassuring smile for Belle, she left for the church.

She also took the empty tea chest.

Everyone was unusually quiet as they ate the reheated stew and bannock Belle had prepared. She also made a big pot of tea and poured it when she served the Saskatoon berry pie she'd found in the pantry. Belle knew the adults were worried about the troubles, but Belle had troubles of her own.

After the dishes had been washed, Belle went up to her room. The more she thought about what she suspected Sarah had done, the more unfair it seemed. Cheating was wrong and so was lying!

Belle had an idea. If she got up very early tomorrow, she could take their canoe across the river, talk to Madame Coteau and be back before breakfast. She was good with a canoe. Her brother Patrice often said she would have made a great voyageur. Coming from Patrice, this was a high compliment indeed! The voyageurs were hearty Metis who used the rivers to explore vast tracks of unexplored land as they hunted for furs. Their canoeing skills were legendary.

Her mother had said she couldn't leave the house for the rest of today, but she had said nothing about tomorrow! Belle climbed into bed feeling better. Tomorrow she would prove that Sarah had cheated in the contest.

10

Secrets Uncovered!

The sun had not crested the horizon when Belle awoke. She dressed in the dark. As she crept downstairs, she was careful to skip the squeaky step. With her woolen sweater buttoned up against the early morning chill, Belle started toward the dock where her father and brother stored the canoe. It would have been easier if the ferry were running, but it was too early and Belle couldn't wait.

Patrice had taught her how to handle the big canoe and use the j-stroke to propel it swiftly and silently. Thinking of Patrice reminded her that today, Saturday, the ninth of May 1885, was his eighteenth birthday. He'd long been waiting for today as he planned to travel with a group of voyageurs from Quebec, but Papa had forbidden him to go until he was eighteen.

She smiled. He was going to be so surprised when she gave him the leather pouch she'd made to carry his valuables in as he paddled across country. A lot of the men tucked articles like a knife or a pipe into the folds of their Metis sashes, but Belle had wanted to make her brother something special.

She pushed the canoe away from the dock, springing into the stern. The big river, high with spring run-off, snatched at the light craft. Belle concentrated on paddling at an angle to the current so that when she reached the other shore, she would still be within walking distance of Madame Coteau's.

The weathered cabin looked run-down and uninviting. An owl flew overhead, its powerful wings beating the air, *whoosh, whoosh, whoosh.*

Belle shivered, remembering the stories about Madame Coteau being an evil witch and children disappearing when they went to her haunted house. She looked back toward the river where she'd beached the canoe. It wasn't too late to forget all this nonsense and go back home.

Then she thought of Marie-Antoinette and how sad she'd sounded when Sarah had practiced ringing her after mass last week. Taking a deep breath, Belle drew herself up, walked to the door and knocked loudly.

Standing there waiting in the cold gray light of the coming dawn, she wished she'd gone to the outhouse before leaving home.

The door creaked open and Madame Coteau peered out at her.

"What on earth do you want at this hour, child?" She pulled the shawl she was wearing a little tighter around her thin shoulders as she swung the door wide. "Come in, come in before you catch your death. You can tell me your story over a hot cup of tea." She glanced sideways at Belle. "And I'm sure there's a story. Children do not eagerly visit my house." She chuckled to herself as she ushered Belle to the hearth where a fire crackled.

Belle was astounded! This wasn't what she had expected! The old woman seemed friendly and the raisin cake she handed Belle smelled delicious.

"I, I need to talk to you about a very important matter," Belle stammered. She took the cup of steaming tea she was offered. "It concerns the embroidered cloth Sarah Johnson had."

"Yes, yes, what about it?" the old woman asked, pouring herself a cup.

"I need to know if you helped Sarah embroider that cloth." Belle waited.

"Me? Help her embroider the cloth?" She shook her head. "No, I didn't help her."

Belle's spirits sank. Sarah had won fair and square and Belle had been wrong.

"I embroidered the entire thing my-self."

"What?" Belle sat up straight.

"Yes, I did. Sarah asked me to embroider a birthday present for her aunt who is ailing. I was only too glad to help. I used to love to sew, but now..." She shrugged. "I have no reason. Was there a problem with the piece?"

Belle had no choice but to tell Madame Coteau what Sarah had really done with the cloth. "Actually, the embroidery was perfect. In fact, it was so perfect that Sarah won a contest with it. A contest where she said she had done the sewing herself."

A frown creased the old woman's already wrinkled forehead. "Oh dear! That will never do!" She shook her head. "No, that will not do at all! Tell me about this contest."

"It was a contest to see who would get to be the bell ringer at the church. Two girls wanted the job, so Father Moulin decided to have an altar-cloth embroidery contest with the winner being the new bell ringer. Sarah's cloth was so beautiful and perfect." Belle looked a little uneasy. "Who would have expected the judges to look at both sides of the cloth. The back was just as beautiful as the front! It was amazing, and...," her voice trailed off, "Sarah was chosen."

A knowing look came into Madame Coteau's sparkling brown eyes. "I'm guessing the other girl in the contest was you." She glanced at Belle's hands and chuckled.

They were rough and callused and could have easily belonged to a boy. "And I'd say needlework is not your favorite thing to do."

Belle blushed furiously. "I tried my best. My mother thought I had done a very good job considering I didn't know the difference between a French knot and a satin stitch before this all began."

"And now?" Madame Coteau refilled Belle's cup.

"And now I know at least a dozen stitches, their names and how to use them properly to make my flowers come to life!" She grinned, realizing as she spoke how much she had enjoyed the project. "I've been thinking of trying my hand at a pillowcase to go with the new quilt my mama is making for my bed." She heard the enthusiasm in her voice and suddenly felt a little shy.

"And this Sarah? Does she sew?" The gray-haired woman rose and went to the fire, adding another log to the blaze.

"Sarah doesn't believe she should have to do menial tasks like cleaning and sewing. That's what made me suspicious in the first place. She says she wouldn't be caught dead grubbing around doing domestic chores, then she hands in a cloth so perfect that the angels could find no mistakes."

"Thank you for the compliment, my child. I think what Sarah did was unfair. I will write you a note to take to Father Moulin explaining everything." She went to an old wooden table and took out a pen and ink. In an elegant hand, she wrote a letter explaining what had happened.

"Congratulations!" she said, handing Belle the folded note. "I believe you are now the winner of the contest. One day, I hope to come back and perhaps see your work on display at the church."

"Come back?" It was then that Belle noticed the trunks and bags piled around the room. "Are you leaving Batoche?" she asked.

"Yes. I'm afraid with all the troubles, my family has decided it is too dangerous for me to live out here alone. My son is coming this morning and I will go to live with him in Regina." She shuffled over to a well-worn trunk and opened the lid.

Reaching inside she removed the most beautiful thing Belle had ever seen. It was a fabulously embroidered red silk bag. She held it out to Belle.

"Take it, child! I want you to have it." The old lady chuckled. "A parting gift from the witch who lives in the haunted house."

Belle reached for the braided cord from which the extraordinary bag was suspended. The scenes looked like pictures Belle had seen once in a book from China. Clouds swirled around the peaks of lofty mountains and strange looking houses with curved roofs nestled in valleys. Delicate ladies wore long dresses with wide sleeves. The details were so exact that Belle could see the exotic tilt of the ladies' eyes as they hid their faces behind decorative fans.

"Did you make this?" she asked in a whisper.

"Yes, a long time ago. I think someone who is just learning to sew should understand that embroidery is not just a chore, but an art. If you look inside, there is a set of tools to help you." Madame Coteau nodded for Belle to look.

Belle reached into the silken bag and withdrew a small pair of scissors shaped like a tall bird, a magnifying glass set in silver and an ornate silver needle case with five golden needles. She drew in her breath. "Oh, Madame! I couldn't!" Belle protested.

"Nonsense, child! Now run along. I must finish my packing." Madame Coteau escorted Belle to the door.

"Merci beaucoup, thank you, Madame, and bonne chance, good luck!" Belle tucked the note she'd been given into the beautiful bag, slung the strap over her shoulder and waved good-bye to the fragile old woman framed in the doorway.

Belle had nearly reached the canoe when she thought of how surprised her mother would be when she saw the beautiful bag!

Her mother! Belle looked up at the sun, now well above the horizon. It was late! She hadn't meant to stay so long. It must be after eight o'clock, way past breakfast, and her mother must know by now that she had slipped out. How was she going to explain?

Belle stopped, listening intently as an unfamiliar sound drifted to her on the early morning breeze.

Gunfire!

Batoche was under attack!

11

Attack on Batoche!

Belle's breath caught in her chest. She looked across the river to the south. There, far in the distance, columns of mounted men and foot soldiers moved toward Batoche. It was happening, just as everyone had feared. Batoche was under attack!

But those soldiers were still far away and the gunfire she'd heard was close by. Where was it coming from? As she broke through the willows at the river's edge, she saw it.

A massive steamboat with *Northcote* painted on its prow was heading toward Batoche. The large boat's two decks were fortified to protect the soldiers who were firing at the Metis on the riverbank. Black clouds billowed from its twin smokestacks as it churned up the river.

The Metis fired at the floating fortress. Puffs of smoke rose from the bushes along the shoreline where the defenders were hidden.

Ducking back into the willows, Belle waited until the boat passed, then with shaking hands she pushed her canoe into the water. She must get across the river before the soldiers on the boat spotted her.

The sound of gunfire from the big boat was louder as it came to her over the water. Her mother would be frantic with worry!

The shortest distance was to paddle straight across the river, but when she pointed her canoe at the opposite shore, the current's pull grew much stronger. She focused on paddling, fighting the current with every stroke. She felt rather than saw the canoe tipping. Water splashed over the edge and soaked her dress and the beautiful embroidered bag.

Belle tried to steady her craft. If it were swamped now, she would be an easy target as she struggled to get to shore. She angled the bow slightly, which would take her dangerously close to the stern of the steamboat, but made it easier to control the canoe.

A sudden shriek of tearing metal and yelling from the big boat made her look up. She couldn't believe her eyes.

As the *Northcote* moved upstream, the Metis had lowered the cable that pulled the ferry across the river. The cable had sheared off the twin smokestacks, which had fallen to the deck below. Smoke billowed out of the stricken boat as men ran here and there.

Without the smokestacks, the engines had no power, and the big boat listed and turned out of control as the current tore at the hull, pushing it back downstream.

Belle gasped. The huge boat was heading straight for her!

She paddled frantically as the *Northcote* loomed over her. Pointing the canoe directly across the path of the steamboat, Belle pulled on the paddle with all her might.

Her back ached with the strain. The disabled steamboat drew closer and closer, pushed by the force of the river on its broad hull. With less than a paddle's length separating them, Belle propelled the canoe forward and out of the path of the lumbering giant.

A stray bullet whizzed past her as she reached the shore. She leapt out of the canoe and ran for the cover of the bushes. The shooting was fierce. She had to work her way down the riverbank away from the fighting.

Taking care to keep under the cover of the dense willows, Belle scrambled through the brush, branches tearing at her face and hair. Fear drove her on. Her friends and family were back there fighting, or hurt, or worse.

Belle forced her mind to go blank.

She worked her way south along the riverbank and started to make a wide circle back to Batoche. The column of soldiers was much closer now, and Belle decided to let them pass by before she made her break.

She was astonished at how many men there were. Hundreds and hundreds of soldiers were coming to fight the Metis.

Through the dust rising from their horses, she glimpsed a strange looking weapon that was so large it was mounted on two wheels. The barrel wasn't a single metal tube, but many all joined together in a group and it had a tall rod sticking out of the top filled with bullets. On the side was a crank, which Belle realized would be used to fire the deadly bullets. This was the terrible Gatling gun she had heard about. It could shoot many rounds per minute, and there was no defense against it.

As she made her way to the top of a sharp rise, Belle was surprised to hear voices coming from the other side. Dropping to her knees, she crawled to the edge and peered over.

Below her, three soldiers stood with their horses. One was tightening the cinch on the saddle as his mount skittered nervously. They were all smoking cigars. The smell made Belle think of burning manure.

"McCorry, hurry up! We're falling behind!" growled a tall soldier with a drooping moustache.

"Don't worry, Nattras. When they start firing that nine-pound cannon, there'll be so much confusion, we'll have no trouble taking the bell." He kneed his horse in the belly to get the big mare to blow out her breath, then pulled the cinch tight.

The third man remounted his tall black horse. "Quit jawin' and mount up! We might not be the only ones who know about the silver waiting in that bell tower."

"Who made you boss, Stainthorp?" The one called McCorry laughed, climbing back on his horse. "When we melt that bell down, even split three ways, we'll have more money than we could make in a year in this stinking army."

The three men moved off at a canter as Belle watched, wide-eyed. They could only have been talking about one thing: Marie-Antoinette!

They were going to steal the bell from the church!

12

Hide Out!

Belle looked back toward the river. She could still hear the gunfire, but she had no choice. She would have to go into the heart of the fighting to warn Father Moulin what was going to happen.

Belle scrambled to her feet and ran as fast as she could for Batoche!

Her breath came in ragged gasps as she topped the last hill on the outskirts of the town. She stared in disbelief at the scene below.

Women and children were running everywhere, fleeing the echoing gunfire. The cannon boomed. Where the shells struck, houses exploded as though they were made of matchsticks.

Belle became aware of a smoky haze in the air around her. "Oh no!" she whispered. Directly below her on the riverbank, the Johnson house was on fire! Flames licked the sides of the wooden building, reaching fiery tentacles toward the roof where, to Belle's horror, Sarah clung to the chimney, her brother Samuel slumped beside her.

Belle raced down the hill to the Johnson house.

"Sarah, you and Samuel must get down!" she screamed. "The fire is on the second floor and soon the roof will be gone!"

Sarah sobbed as she gripped the stone chimney for support. "There's no way down!" she cried. "Belle, please help us!"

"Where are your parents?" Belle called back, praying that they were not trapped inside.

"Gone," Sarah wailed. "And the maid ran away when they... when they started shooting."

Her brother Samuel didn't look right to Belle. He wasn't moving. "Is Samuel hurt?" she called up. Why had their parents left them on such a day?

"He was asleep in his room, in all that smoke. He won't wake up." Sarah touched her brother gently on the head. "I think he's going to die!" She began wailing even more loudly.

"Nonsense!" Belle called. "Sarah Johnson, you stop blubbering this minute! Your brother needs you." Belle had to do something quickly. She could see the fire was spreading rapidly. "Where's your ladder?" she shouted, peering around the yard.

"I ... I don't know," Sarah cried, "maybe in the shed at the back."

Belle ran to the shed, but the wooden ladder was too heavy for her to move by herself. She hurried back to Sarah.

"I'm going to get my parents," she shouted. "Hang on!" Belle raced for her house. Please let Mama and Papa be there, she prayed as bullets whined around her and cannon balls exploded. Behind her, soldiers were coming up the road. She ran even faster.

Belle slammed through the back door and gasped with relief. Her mother was right there in the kitchen, packing supplies into an old carpetbag.

"Belle! Thank God!" Her mother rushed to her and gathered Belle in her arms. "Hurry, we must go to the church and hide. Where were you? I looked everywhere!"

"We can't hide, Mama. Sarah's house is on fire. Sarah and Samuel are trapped on the roof. We have to help them." Belle looked into her mother's worried face. "Are Papa and Patrice here?" she asked, but she knew the answer.

"Non, child. They are with the men in the rifle pits." Her mother shook her head, tears in her eyes. "All the men have gone to fight."

Belle paused for only a moment to take in what her mother had told her. Then she grabbed her mother's hand and pulled her toward the door.

"But, Belle, where are their parents? It's not safe!"

"I don't know, Mama!" Belle cried. "We must go." Belle tugged harder at her mother's hand, and at last her mother followed.

When they reached the Johnson's, the air was filled with smoke. Belle and her mother dragged the big wooden ladder from the shed and managed to place it against the side of the burning building.

"Climb down, child!" Belle's mother called up to Sarah, coughing as a gush of smoke billowed out of a downstairs window. Flames licked the edges of the roof, eating through the wooden shingles.

Sarah looked at the ladder, then at her unconscious brother lying beside her on the roof. "I can't leave Samuel!" she shouted. "And he's too big for me to carry!" She started wailing again. Belle wished she would stop.

"Come down and I will get your brother!" Belle's mother said, bracing the bottom of the ladder. She looked up at the flames. "Hurry, Sarah! There's not much time."

Rung by rung, her legs shaking, Sarah climbed down. When she reached the bottom, she stared at Belle. Her eyes looked strange, like someone dreaming. Sarah didn't seem like herself at all.

"Hold the ladder," Belle's mother said as she started up.

Belle grabbed the ladder, but Sarah just stood, looking around blankly until Belle repeated her mother's instructions.

Sarah obeyed her without a word.

Please let Mama reach Samuel in time, Belle prayed as she watched her mother climb through the smoke. She was nearly at the top when a sudden blast of hot air and searing flames exploded out of the two upstairs windows.

Belle sucked in her breath and Sarah screamed as Belle's mother seemed to be caught in the explosion. The ladder swayed, but did not fall. Belle's mother had reached the roof.

Through the thick choking smoke, Belle saw her mother dragging Samuel across the roof then holding him against her shoulder as she started back down past the wall of flames.

She had just reached the bottom when, with a loud roar the roof collapsed, sending a shower of sparks and cinders high into the air.

"We must get to shelter, quickly!" Belle's mother said, still holding the unmoving Samuel. Her arms and hands were black with soot and the sleeves of her dress were in scorched tatters.

Through the gunfire and constant shelling, they started back to Belle's house, but before they could reach it, they saw soldiers riding toward them.

Belle looked around. There were troops closing in from all directions. They had nowhere to run to, nowhere to hide! She glanced back at her mother, struggling to carry Samuel, and Sarah who still seemed dazed.

She had an inspiration. "Come with me!" she shouted, turning to follow the trail that skirted the river. Her mother and Sarah hurried after her as she raced through the willows. As they ran, Belle kept a constant eye out for the government troops. When she had gone some distance along the path, Belle began looking for the hard to find spot on the hillside.

"Where are we going?" Sarah asked.

Belle heard the fear in Sarah's voice. "Someplace safe!" She tried to sound confident, but knew the soldiers were closing in. They had only moments before they would be seen crossing the prairie. Gunfire echoed in her ears and she could smell smoke from the burning buildings. With a burst of speed, Belle sprinted across the open grass and scrambled up the side of the steep embankment.

She smiled with satisfaction as she spotted what she'd been looking for: the old root cellar door.

"Sarah, help me!" she said, tugging on the weathered wooden handle.

Belle and Sarah pulled with all their might until, with a groan, the door opened. "Quickly, go inside!" she instructed Sarah.

"But it's dirty and dark and there's probably spiders!" Sarah whimpered, sounding like a young child.

"There's a lot worse than that out here! Go on, Sarah, I'm right behind you!" Belle gave Sarah a gentle push that sent her tumbling into the dark root cellar. Belle's mother followed, Samuel still in her arms.

With one last look at the terrible battle taking place in her peaceful little town, Belle pulled the heavy door closed behind her.

13

Belle Takes Charge

The root cellar was dark and still damp with the late thawing ground. Belle was surprised at how large the man-made cave was.

"Are root cellars usually this big, Mama?" she asked, peering around in the gloom. She saw Sarah sitting, hugging her knees to her chest and rocking quietly back and forth.

Her mother placed Samuel gently on the ground. She inspected her surroundings. "This must be the old Belanger place. I remember the family moved to Batoche late in the year and had to live in the root cellar the first winter because they couldn't build a house until spring. I had no idea this still existed."

Belle, busily snooping at the back of the dim cellar, discovered an old rusty lantern. She shook it. "It still has a little oil. Now all we need is a way of lighting it!" Then she remembered the small leather bag her mother kept tied to her belt. "Do you have your flint and steel?"

"Take the pouch," her mother instructed.

Belle thought this was odd, but did as she was instructed, untying the soft deer-skin bag from her mother's belt.

Easing the glass chimney off the lantern, Belle laid it on the ground, then rummaged in the pouch, withdrawing the steel and flint. "If I do this right, we should be able to see, at least." Belle struck the flint against the steel, sending a shower of sparks onto the oil-soaked wick.

A small ember flickered to life, then the wick flared. The glow from the old lantern bathed Belle's face as she replaced the chimney. Smiling, she looked up at her mother and stopped.

"Mama, what's the matter?" she asked, noticing how her mother held her hands away from her body.

"It's nothing, Belle. When I was rescuing Samuel from the roof, my hands were burnt a little." Her voice was light, but Belle saw the sweat on her mother's forehead.

Belle lifted the lantern and looked closely at her mother's hands. "Oh, Mama!" she gasped, noting the red blisters and raw open patches where the skin was entirely burnt away. "We must do something." She looked into her mother's eyes, seeing the agony there. "I must go for the doctor!" she whispered, but they both knew that was not possible.

Sarah got up and moved closer to the light so that she could see Madame Tourond's hands. "This is terrible," she moaned. "Who will take care of us if your hands are all burnt?" She began crying again. "I want my mama and papa. They will know what to do."

Belle took a deep breath. She looked from Sarah's red, tear-stained face, to little Samuel on the floor and then to her mother. She could see her mother biting back the pain.

She remembered her mother's words: One day, you will have no choice, Belle. People will be counting on you. She straightened up, feeling strangely older and somehow, stronger.

"Sarah, stop that crying or I will throw you out for the soldiers to use for target practice!" Shocked, Sarah abruptly shut up. Belle's voice softened. "I'm sorry. I didn't mean that. We have to work together now. You and I are going to take care of my mama and Samuel." She thought Sarah was going to protest, but all she did was nod her head.

Belle checked on Samuel. His breathing was strained. "Samuel!" she called, shaking him. "Samuel, wake up!" But the small boy didn't respond. "Sarah, come and watch over your brother. If he wakes, call me."

Still sniffing, Sarah sat beside her brother.

Belle moved around the cellar using the lantern to check into dark corners for any other treasures that may have been overlooked. There wasn't much left in the old cellar, but she did find a tattered blanket to put over Samuel.

"Mama, you have to have medicine for your hands, and we'll need supplies if we're going to stay here." She couldn't believe that she was saying these things to her mother.

Her mother smiled reassuringly at her, but the corners of her mouth were pinched. "I know, Belle. But we cannot go out into the fighting. It's too dangerous. You could be injured or..." Her voice trailed off.

Belle knew her mother was thinking about Papa and Patrice. She was worried too, but she couldn't let that stop her. She thought for a moment. There was only one way. "Later tonight, when it is dark, I'm going back to our house and gather what we need. It's not far, and I'll be very careful."

She and her mother looked at each other. They both knew if they were to stay hiding here, they would have to have food and water.

"Are you sure you can do it?" her mother asked.

Belle smiled confidently. "Of course I can! I know every inch of prairie around here and, thanks to always being late getting home, I also know every shortcut to our house."

As the afternoon wore on, Belle sat on the cold ground, waiting for nightfall. Her mother was resting, but her hands were now oozing a foul fluid.

Sarah, who had been pacing the dirt floor, became more anxious as the hours dragged by. "We can't possibly stay here. It's not safe. There's no food, and Samuel needs a doctor." She seemed to be talking to herself, and then she looked over at Belle. "How are we going to live in this oversized gopher hole? We should have waited for my parents."

Belle looked up at Sarah. "And where would you have waited? The last time I looked there wasn't much left of your house."

Sarah opened her mouth to say something more, but instead, she went to check on her brother. After a while, she straightened up and stomped back over to Belle. "My parents went to Duck Lake on business very early this morning before all this, this ... " She waved her arm in the direction of the cellar door. "This craziness began. They weren't coming back until tomorrow, but what if they heard about the fighting and tried to return for us? They could be caught in the gunfire!"

Belle heard the panic in Sarah' s voice. "Your papa is a smart man. He wouldn't walk into the middle of a battle. I'm sure he and your mother are safe. They're probably waiting for the troops to leave so he can come for you and Samuel."

Sarah thought about this for a minute and seemed to be satisfied. She was much calmer as she went back to sit with her unconscious brother.

The hours dragged slowly by until finally Belle stretched and got up. "Mama, I think it's time. I'm going to go now." She tried to sound brave.

"I wish there was another way, ma cherie, but there is none. Please, please be careful, Belle."

As Belle hugged her mother, she noticed her burnt hands had now curled up into claws and the skin was a strange color.

"I won't be long, Mama." She made her voice light as she went to the old door. "Don't go anywhere without me!"

Belle slipped into the velvet darkness outside. The night was still and very quiet. She could hear the frogs croaking down by the river's edge. Carefully, she inspected the root cellar door to make sure no light could be seen leaking out around the cracks. Satisfied no telltale clue would alert soldiers as to where they were, Belle stealthily started making her way back to her house.

As she moved through the inky blackness, Belle was startled when she heard movement in the darkness ahead. She scurried away being careful to avoid getting any closer to where the sounds had come from. Pushing through the bushes, she could see campfires dotting the surrounding countryside. They must be government troops. The Metis would never be so foolish as to give their positions away by lighting fires.

The tall grass felt cold on her legs as she made her way along the edge of the embankment. She kept low to the ground so her silhouette couldn't be seen against the moonlit skyline. Belle was glad for all those days spent exploring every inch of this vast open area around Batoche. She knew every boulder and bush between her and her family's cozy little house. At last, she could see her home not far ahead.

Checking first to make sure no one had been alerted to her movements, she ran across the open ground to the back door.

Her heart pounded as she pressed her body against the side of the house. Belle listened for any sound of soldiers. Satisfied that the house was empty, she crept inside.

It was as black as pitch. In the dark, Belle moved through the familiar rooms gathering the items they would need.

As quickly as possible, she found blankets, bannock and dried meat and piled them on the kitchen table. She would have to use the pump in the sink to fill the skin water bags. When she moved the cast iron handle up and down to draw the water, the pump screeched its annoyance.

Belle cringed. She hoped no soldiers were passing close enough to hear.

After filling the water bags, she grabbed her mother's medicine pouch, which contained bandages, herbs and several of her mother's favorite medicines. She reached into the bag and smiled as her fingers closed around the old glass jar with the special salve her mother had used when Belle had burnt her foot. She tucked the medicine pouch and all her other treasures into the carpetbag that her mother had been packing, added another lantern for good measure and slipped back out into the night.

Soundlessly, she made her way back toward the root cellar. Just as she was going to make a dash to the hidden door, a mounted patrol rounded a small hill and headed straight for her. Belle dropped to the ground and lay flat, hoping the grass was tall enough to hide her. The sound of the horses' hooves came closer and closer. Staying perfectly still, she held her breath as the two men passed. Still not daring to move, she watched them until they disappeared around the next hill, then scrambling to her feet, she ran for the root cellar.

When she reached the old door, she was careful to close it securely behind her. With the soldiers so close, she wasn't taking any chances.

"Belle! Thank heavens!" Her mother was still sitting in the same place. Her face looked very white in the pale light cast by the old lantern.

"I had no trouble," Belle said, not bothering to mention the patrol. She unloaded her supplies and lit the second lantern. "This will give us more light and," she grinned at Sarah, "take the chill off our oversized gopher hole."

Belle walked over to her mother with the bandages and salve. "I hope this will ease the pain." She held the medicine out to her mother, then realized that wouldn't work. Her mother's hands were too damaged. "Tell me what to do, Mama."

Her mother smiled at her. "Oui, ma petite fille, we begin ..." Her mother told her what to do, and Belle set to work cleaning her mother's burns and applying the sooth-ing salve. She was careful to keep the ban-dages loose so that she could remove them easily. She knew from the way the burns were still weeping that the bandages would need changing by morning.

"That is perfect, Belle. You did a fine job." Her mother looked tired as Belle returned the medicine and bandages to the pouch.

"Does it hurt much?" she asked, looking at the bandages.

"It is much better now. Merci, cherie." Her mother closed her eyes and leaned back against the wall. Belle went over to where Sarah sat next to her brother. "How's he doing?" she asked, feeling the little boy's forehead.

"He's the same." Sarah looked at Belle with fear in her eyes. "Is he going to die?" she asked.

Belle heard the quaver in her voice. "Of course not!" she said firmly. "We're going to nurse him back to health." She poured cool water into an old bowl, soaked a cloth in it and handed Sarah the cloth. "Put this on his forehead and talk to him. When our horses are sick, my Papa speaks to them and tells them everything is going to be alright, and you know what?"

Sarah shook her head.

"Everything usually is! I think horses and little brothers like being fussed over and talked to."

She left Sarah cooing to her brother and went to the old carpetbag. Pulling the food and blankets out, Belle gave some of each to Sarah and tucked two extra blankets around Samuel. After this, she busied herself feeding her mother bits of bannock and meat and offering sips of water.

When she finally turned the lantern out, she was very very tired.

14

Living in a Gopher Hole

As near as Belle could tell, it was just after noon on their second day in the root cellar. She had changed the dressing on her mother's hands, and though they still looked terrible, her mother didn't think the infection was getting worse.

As the afternoon worn on, the noise of the guns became constant and the strain was very hard to take. Samuel had fallen into a feverish sleep, tossing and turning fitfully as his breathing became raspy.

Sarah hovered over her brother, jumping up and down, replacing the cloth on his forehead and peering at his pale, still face.

Belle could understand her concern. If that had been her brother Patrice, she would have been worried too. Thinking of Patrice made the knot in her stomach tighten. Please let Patrice and Papa be all right, she prayed. She gave her body a shake. When she spoke, her voice was soft. "Let him rest, Sarah. Your fussing is wearing me out."

Sarah's chin wobbled. "This is all my fault," she said.

Belle was confused. "Why? You didn't set your house on fire."

Sarah shook her head. "No, you don't understand. After mother and father left, Samuel began complaining that he felt sickly. I thought he was just being a baby and I teased him." She wiped at her face. "But he's always getting sick. Mother says it's because when he was a baby he had the croup and it left him weak. I should have sent for the doctor this morning. Maybe the smoke wouldn't have made him so sick."

"Sarah," Belle said softly, "even if the doctor had come in the morning, the smoke would still have made Samuel much worse."

"I suppose you're right, Belle. It's just that I feel so helpless." Sarah sniffed loudly.

"Me too, Sarah. But we can't fight bullets with our bare hands." Belle smiled. "I'm sure Samuel knows you're taking good care of him."

As the day wore on, Belle's mother kept checking on the little boy's condition. When afternoon came, she laid her head gently on Samuel's chest and listened to his breathing. She shook her head. "I'm afraid he may be developing pneumonia. We must keep him warm."

They had been using only one lantern turned very low to save the fuel, but now Belle lit the second lantern and turned both up as high as she safely could. She moved the lanterns closer to Samuel and took Sarah's blanket and wrapped it around the small figure.

Belle had thought Sarah would protest, but she handed the blanket over without a word.

"With only my blanket for the two of us, you and I are going to be blanket buddies," Belle said, hoping to cheer Sarah up. She could see that Sarah was still afraid for her brother. She thought of her papa and

Patrice and swallowed the fear that made her throat feel so tight. As evening drew in, Belle decided she should change her mother's bandages again before they turned in for the night.

Sarah was huddled in the corner, not saying a word as she tossed small stones across the cellar, trying to hit an old bucket that was leaning against the wall.

"Sarah, come and help me, please." Belle needed more light to work on her mother's burns.

"I don't know anything about fixing burnt up hands," Sarah said as she tossed another rock.

"Then that makes two of us. Your job will be to hold the lantern, so I can see what I'm doing, and hand me the salve and bandages when I need them." Belle eased off the soaked bandages and listened as her mother told her what to do to dress the burns.

"I think I may faint!" Sarah said in a whispery voice, staring wide-eyed at the raw wounds.

Belle looked at her. "I need your help,

Sarah." Her voice was calm although her own stomach was feeling queasy.

"I'm proud of you girls being such wonderful young nurses," Belle's mother said, smiling, but Belle heard the strain in her voice. "I know this is very hard for you both."

They had just finished the bandaging when they heard a low rumbling. It began far away, then became louder and louder. Finally, the pounding was directly over their heads. The ground shook and dust rained down on them. Belle was afraid the roof was going to cave in.

"It's horses, lots of them." Belle's mother looked up at the ceiling of the root cellar. "And they are right on top of us."

"Maybe it's our families looking for us!" Sarah clapped her hands, her eyes wild with hope.

"Maybe, but I don't think so." Belle turned the lanterns down and went to the door, opening it a small crack. She listened, then closed it again. "It's a group of redcoats and they're setting up camp for the night. We must be very quiet!" she whispered.

Even in the dim light, Belle could see Sarah's face grow pale.

"It's late and we were going to sleep anyway," she said reassuringly. "As long as they don't keep us awake, we'll have no trouble with them." Belle offered Sarah her blanket. "Why don't you sleep beside Samuel? I'm sure he'll feel better with you near."

Sarah took the blanket and went over to her brother.

Belle cuddled up next to her mother, but whether it was from cold or worry, she found she couldn't sleep.

Toward dawn, Samuel began to cough.

Belle sat up, stiff with fear. "Mama, do you have anything in your medicine bag to ease Samuel's coughing?" she asked. Her mother followed Belle's gaze to the ceiling. If the soldiers heard…

Her mother thought for a moment. "I have just the thing," she said. "Quick, bring me my bag."

Belle did as she was told.

"Look for a small vial of honey and lemon mixture."

Belle rummaged in the medicine pouch, then with a grin, pulled out the slim bottle. "I know what to do with this."

Mixing a dollop into a cup with water, she held it to Samuel's parched lips. Even in his delirious state, he drank the sweet soothing liquid greedily.

Belle gently pushed his damp hair off the small boy's forehead, then sighed. His breathing had eased and he had stopped coughing for the moment.

"I'm too hot," Sarah whispered. She'd been watching Belle tend to her brother. "Why don't you take the blanket and try to get some sleep? I'll watch Samuel." She held the blanket out to Belle.

Belle was sure Sarah wasn't too hot at all, as the root cellar was very chilly. Exhaustion washed over her in a dark wave. Nodding, she took the blanket. "Thanks."

Later, Belle became aware of Sarah huddled beside her. "You're keeping me awake with your shivering," she whispered and wrapped the blanket around them both. In minutes, they were fast asleep.

They were awoken the next morning by the sounds of men and horses moving about. Soon the noises stopped and Belle edged the door open. Climbing carefully up to the side of the embankment, she peeked over the top. The soldiers had broken camp and were gone. Belle scrambled back to the cellar to tell the others. They spent the day talking and telling stories. Belle's mother made the girls laugh with her tales of how things were done in the old days. As the noise of the battle continued, Belle and Sarah sang songs to keep their spirits up.

"You have a nice voice," Belle said as Sarah finished singing an old lullaby her grandmother had taught her.

"Really?" Sarah said, surprised. "My mother always complained I couldn't carry a tune in a bucket."

"Is that why you never joined the choir?" Belle asked.

Sarah looked uncomfortable, then she giggled. "Actually, my mother said I shouldn't mix with riff raff."

Belle looked at her, then started giggling

too. "Well, if you ever find this Riff Raff fellow, let me know because I'm sure I don't want to mix with him either!"

That night, Belle stole back out to her house for more supplies. It was a disappointing trip as soldiers had broken in and taken nearly all the remaining food, leaving only some stale bannock and a couple of pieces of salt pork.

When she returned to the cellar, Belle was surprised to see her mother and Sarah hovering over Samuel. Belle feared the worst.

"His fever is very high," her mother said, looking up. The worry in her face was plain. "We need to lower his temperature."

The three of them took turns through the night sponging Samuel down. As Belle fell into a fitful doze, she heard her mother whispering a prayer for all of them to live through this terrible time.

Belle was the last to take her turn and was still awake when Tuesday morning arrived. Samuel was coughing again, but she thought it sounded better than the day before.

As she set out the last of the bannock and jam she wondered where she could go for more food if the battle didn't end soon.

"Will those terrible guns never stop!" Sarah grumbled, unwrapping herself from the blanket. "I can't stand it anymore."

Belle understood how Sarah felt. The cannon fire had started early and it now seemed louder than ever. "Try to think of something pleasant," Belle suggested. "Like the new hat your parents will buy you when they find out the last one is a little pile of ashes in a bigger pile of ashes."

Sarah sighed and pursed her lips. "You're right. In fact, I think my parents should buy us both new hats since we had to spend four days in this oversized rabbit burrow."

"Are we in a real rabbit burrow?" A small voice asked.

"Samuel, you're awake!" Sarah gasped.

Belle hurried over to the boy and felt his head. "His fever's gone!"

Samuel looked around, then smiled weakly up at Belle. "It looks more like a gopher hole."

Belle laughed. "That's what your sister thought too!"

"Welcome back, petit fils," Belle's mother nodded. "You gave us quite a scare." She was able to move her hands a little and the horrible oozing had stopped.

"This is wonderful!" Belle hugged Sarah. "Since Samuel finally woke up and joined our party, he will get the last of the Saskatoon jam!"

"And both our pieces of bannock!" Sarah laughed, hugging Belle back.

It was at this moment that Belle noticed something odd. "Shh!" she hissed. "Listen!"

They all stopped and listened.

"I don't hear anything," Sarah said, frowning.

"Exactly!" Belle ran over to the door. "No guns!" She pushed the door wide open and looked out.

15

Battle's End and a Friendship Begun

Belle couldn't believe her eyes. Her whole world had changed.

Below her lay Batoche, or what was left of Batoche. Some houses and stores had big gaping holes where the cannonballs had hit and others had boards ripped apart from the Gatling gun. Windows were broken and fire had destroyed several buildings.

Soldiers were everywhere, and Belle could see groups of Metis men being marched away under guard. Her heart sank.

The Metis had lost the battle.

Belle's mother came and stood silently beside her surveying the devastation. "We must go and find your papa and Patrice!"

She was looking toward the men who were under arrest. "It is such a sad thing to hope to see them with the prisoners."

Belle knew her mother was thinking of all the men who must have been killed in the fighting. She put her arm around her mother's waist. "Don't worry, Mama. They are safe. I know it."

Her mother reached out one bandaged hand and touched Belle's cheek. "I want you to know how proud I am of you, ma petite fille. These last terrible days, you have shown me that you are growing up and when you need to, you can take care of not only yourself, but those around you."

A tear squeezed out of the corner of Belle's eye. "Oh, Mama. I love you!" They hugged each other, and Belle noticed for the first time that she was nearly as tall as her mother.

Her mother smiled at her. "Come now, we must go and see if we can find your papa so that I can tell him about his wonderful daughter."

They gathered their belongings, and with Sarah supporting her little brother, the small group started back to Batoche. Belle was the last to leave the old root cellar where they had sheltered. Their world would be different now and she knew it. Slinging her beautiful embroidered bag over her shoulder, she hurried after the small group as they made their way down the gently sloping hill.

Father Moulin was leaning on a stick when they found him in front of what was left of Monsieur Letendre's store. He said he'd been shot in the leg by a stray bullet. A group of weary looking women and children stood with the priest, and across the street Belle saw Sarah's parents. Mr. Johnson had his arm around Sarah's mother, and Belle thought he looked very tired. His clothes were dusty as though the couple had traveled a long way. Sarah's mother looked worse. Her dress was muddy and the brim of her fine hat was torn and dangled at an odd angle. Belle nudged Sarah and pointed.

Sarah waved excitedly. "Mama! Papa! Over here!"

Sarah's father saw her first and his face broke into a wide smile of delight, then Mrs. Johnson looked in their direction and began frantically waving her handkerchief. With cries of joy, the parents rushed over to their two children. "Sarah! Samuel! Thank heaven!" Sarah's father scooped Samuel up in his arms while Sarah's mother began crying and hugging her daughter.

"We only returned from Duck Lake this morning," Sarah's father explained. "The soldiers would not let us come back any earlier. We have been frantic with worry. Where were you all this time?"

Amid hugs and exclamations of relief, Belle's mother explained what had happened and how they had hidden for the four days of the battle.

Father Moulin hobbled over to where Belle's mother was talking with Sarah's parents. "Madame Tourond, do not worry, your husband and son escaped. They have gone into hiding, but will return once everything quiets down and our visitors have left." The old priest nodded toward the soldiers.

Belle could see relief flood her mother at this news. "Perhaps not all is lost."

"You are sure they are not hurt?" Belle pressed. She wanted Father Moulin to say that her papa and brother were all right. If a priest said they were unhurt, it would be the truth, and the terrible fear she had been carrying would be gone.

Father Moulin nodded. "Do not worry, little one. I saw them ride away with my own eyes."

The tears that Belle had been holding back slid down her cheeks, but she didn't care. Now they were tears of relief. She hugged her mother. "They will be home soon, Mama. I know it!"

"I'm sure you are right, ma fille." Her mother smiled and Belle saw the love shining in her eyes. Her voice sounded sad to Belle, but she thought she heard a hopeful note also.

As the grown-ups discussed what they would do next, Belle and Sarah listened quietly. Suddenly Belle remembered the soldiers who had said they were going to steal Marie-Antoinette. Perhaps they had not succeeded. Perhaps the bell was still hanging safely in the tower, ready to call everyone to mass on Sunday.

"Sarah, come on! We have to go to the church!" Belle grabbed Sarah's hand and began running.

"What is it?" Sarah asked, trying to keep up.

"I'll explain when we get there!" Belle ran through the burnt-out town and up the hill to the church and then stopped.

Staring up at the bell tower, she felt tears stinging her eyes. "We are too late!"

Sarah looked up, at first confused, then astonished as she too saw the empty tower. "The bell is gone! Someone has stolen Marie-Antoinette!"

"I overheard three soldiers say they were going to steal the bell, but before I could tell anyone, things happened." She shook her head, then felt ashamed at being so sad over a stolen bell when many families had lost everything. Perhaps one day, when peace came to Batoche, they would get Marie-Antoinette back.

She took a deep breath. A lot of things had happened, but not all of them had

been bad. One unexpected good thing Belle had discovered was that sometime over the last four days, Sarah had stopped being annoying and had become a friend.

"Oh, Belle! This ruins everything!" Sarah blurted out and then started crying.

Belle felt bad for her new friend who would never get to be the bell ringer at St. Antoine de Padoue, the most wonderful job in the world.

"Stop belly aching." She nudged Sarah in the ribs. "I'll never get to be the bell ringer either."

Sarah started crying harder. "You don't understand. The contest, I…" She sniffed loudly. "I sort of cheated to win. You were right about Madame Coteau. I did have her embroider the cloth." She dropped to the ground and buried her head in her hands.

Belle sat down beside her. "I know. I went to Madame Coteau's and she told me everything. I even have proof." Belle reached into the embroidered bag and withdrew a wad of paper. She unfolded the note.

Sarah looked up, confused. "You knew? Why didn't you say anything?"

"Because there were more important things going on, and besides, when the time was right, I had my proof. At least I thought I had my proof." She handed the note to Sarah.

Sarah glanced at the paper, then looked at Belle and frowned. "There's nothing but black streaks on this paper."

Belle started laughing. "It was a letter from Madame Coteau to Father Moulin telling him that she embroidered the cloth. I guess when I was canoeing back across the river, it must have become wet and the ink washed away. I can't get another because Madame Coteau has left Batoche. This means your secret is safe." Belle smiled ruefully. "I'm not going to tell because it doesn't matter anymore. Marie-Antoinette has been kidnapped."

Sarah shook her head adamantly. "But it does matter, Belle Tourond. You won that contest fair and square. My secret may be safe with you, but it's not going to remain a secret much longer."

She stood up excitedly. "That was what I meant when I said that everything was ruined. I was going to go to Father Moulin and tell him what I did and that you are the true bell ringer. I was also going to my parents and tell them how the girl they thought was riff raff was the honest one and their lovely daughter was the sneaky snake!" She went on in a rush. "I'm still going to tell the truth because, well…" Her face flushed. "I think we've become friends these last few days and I don't want anything to get in our way. That is, if you still want to be friends with me after what I did…" Her voice trailed off.

Belle looked at the empty bell tower, then back at the ruins of Batoche, now silhouetted in the early evening light. "I think we have a big job ahead of us. It would sure be nice to have a friend by my side while we rebuild Batoche." She grinned at Sarah. "And I know my mama will have a very long list of chores that you could help me with!"

As the gentle twilight wrapped around them, the two new friends smiled at each other and together started walking back through the tall prairie grass toward their home.

Author's Note

Whereas Belle, Sarah and the embroidery contest are fictional, the historical events in this story are based on fact. Batoche was attacked by General Middleton, acting on behalf of Prime Minister John A. Macdonald on Saturday, May 9, 1885; the *Northcote* was disabled by the Metis defenders lowering a ferry cable; Father Moulin was shot in the leg; and the rebellion did end on Tuesday, May 12, 1885.

Marie-Antoinette was the christened name of the twenty-pound silver bell given to St. Antoine du Padoue church by Bishop Grandin. The bell bears the inscription: "Vital-Justin Grandin, Eveque de St. Albert" and had Xavier Letendre dit Batoche, the founder of Batoche, and his sister Marie Letendre-Champagne as godparents.

Marie-Antoinette was stolen during the rebellion by three Millbrook Orangemen named McCorry, Stainthorp and Nattras, and is still missing today.

The Tourond family is real, with changes made to allow this story to be written. The entire family took part in the Rebellion. One son was on Louis Riel's council, and because the family had harbored the rebel leader, the Tourond house was burnt to the ground. Josephte Tourond, a widow, lost two sons in the battle; one more was critically wounded; and two others were captured and taken to Regina for trial. One of them was my great-grandfather, Patrice Tourond.

Acknowledgments

I would like to acknowledge the Canada Council for the Arts and the Alberta Foundation for the Arts for their support while I was writing this book.

Jacqueline Guest is a Metis writer who lives in a log cabin nestled in the pinewoods of the Rocky Mountain foothills of Alberta. She is the author of many other books for children, but *Belle of Batoche* is her first story to incorporate family history and her first book for Orca Book Publishers.

You can find out more about Jacqueline and her stories through her website: www.jacquelineguest.com